THE WINTER NOISY BOOK

BY MARGARET WISE BROWN

PICTURES BY CHARLES G. SHAW

HarperCollins*Publishers*

ISBN 0-06-020865-1. — ISBN 0-06-020866-X (lib. bdg.)
ISBN 0-06-443004-9 (pbk.)
Library of Congress Catalog Card Number 92-46880
New Edition, 1994.
❖

One day a little dog named Muffin saw
all the leaves fall off the trees and blow
away.

He heard the last cricket chirp.
He heard the last butterfly fly by.

And he saw an enormous round red
moon rise over the hill.

Now there were no more green leaves and no more yellow leaves.

Only the night, cold and still, beyond the windows.

Black branches rattled against the windowpane. And always there was the hollow sound of the wind.

And the rain fell in big drops, down.

Then from far away up the road

Thud Thud Thud

Scrunch Scrunch Scrunch

What was that?

The people were coming home.

Muffin was upstairs and
heard them downstairs.

He heard
        click
        (someone turned
            on the light)
He heard
        ha ha ha Ho Ho
        (someone laughed)

He heard
    clink
(someone dropped
a nickel)

He heard
    b-r-r-r-r-r
(someone shook and
shivered and blew his nose)

And outdoors beyond the window he heard a round hissing sound turn over and over in the road, with two big headlights in front of it.

What was that?
And far off
down the

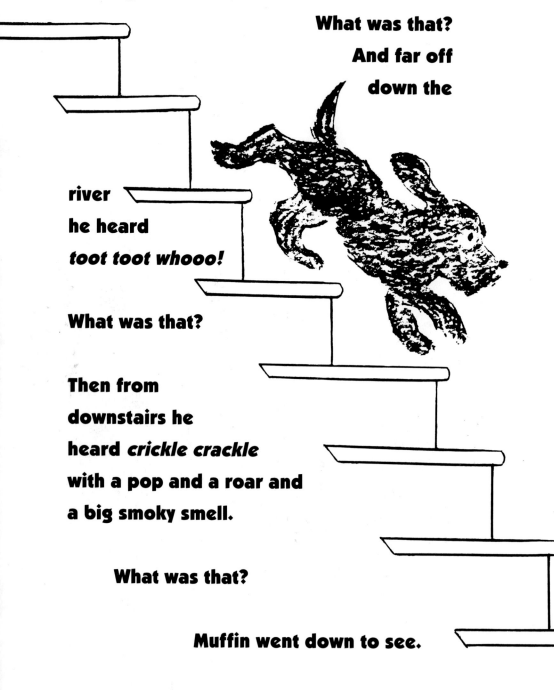

river
he heard
toot toot whooo!

What was that?

Then from
downstairs he
heard *crickle crackle*
with a pop and a roar and
a big smoky smell.

What was that?

Muffin went down to see.

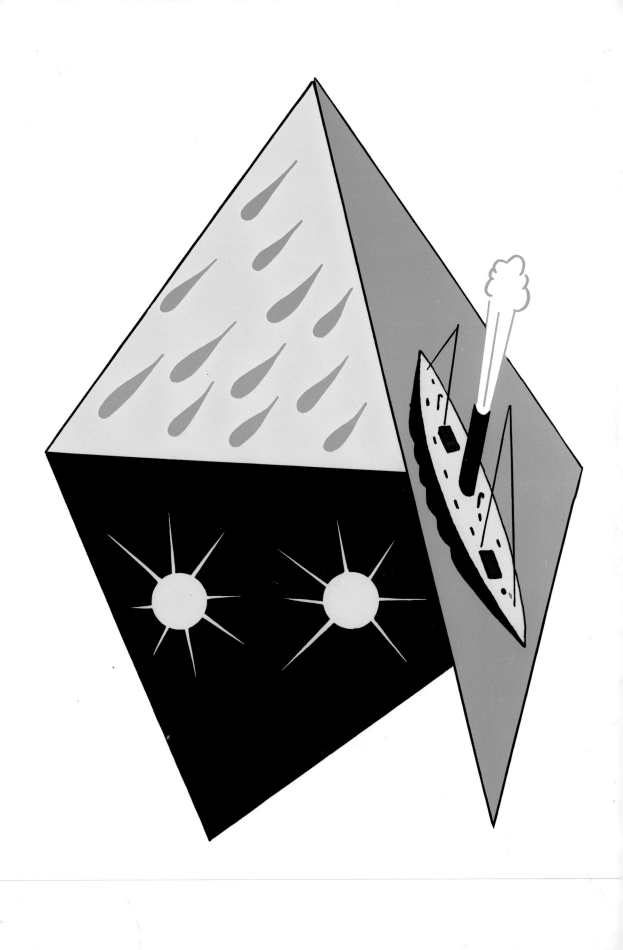

It was a great fire roaring in the fireplace. A big, warm, hot, yellow, roaring fire.

And everybody said, "Here is the little dog Muffin. Let him come and warm his nose at the fire."

And Muffin lay down by the fire and listened to the people crack nuts and eat apples and pop popcorn.

Someone was eating celery.

And a man smoked a pipe.

And a black cat was lying
on a fur rug.

And the frost outside crept
over the windowpane.

But could Muffin hear that?

The next morning Muffin walked out into a shining world of glass. As his little black paws stepped on the green glass grass, there was a tinkling sound. What was that?

The lake was still and shining cold. Could Muffin hear waves splashing?

No. But he walked on the lake and he heard a crack like a gun. What was that?

Could he smell Christmas trees?

No. Because they were all frozen in ice.

And then he heard the most sudden sound in winter—

crack-snap!

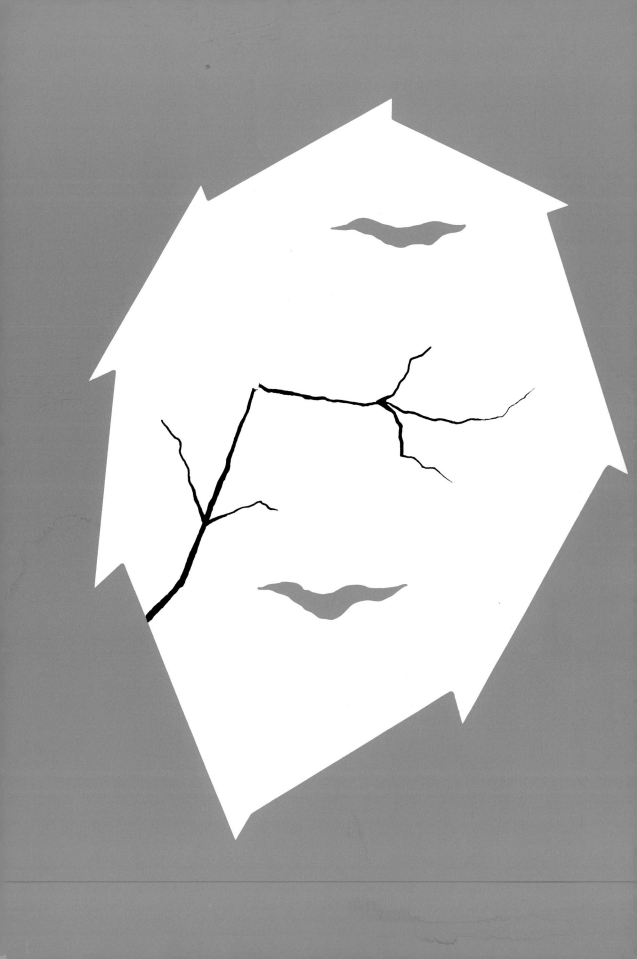

It was not the radiator.

It was not the sun going down.

What could it be?

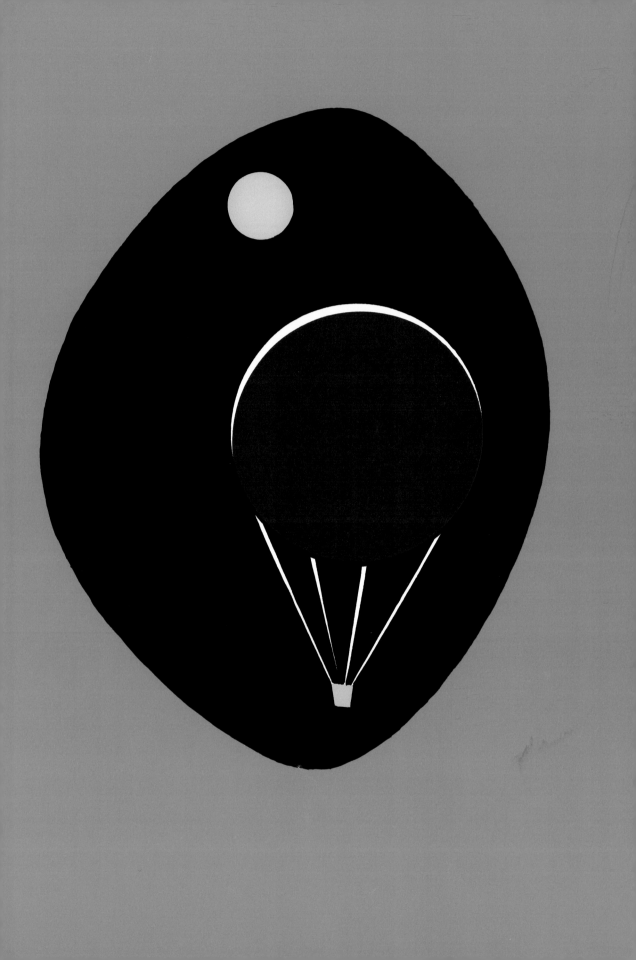

Was it a big balloon going up to the moon?

NO

Was it

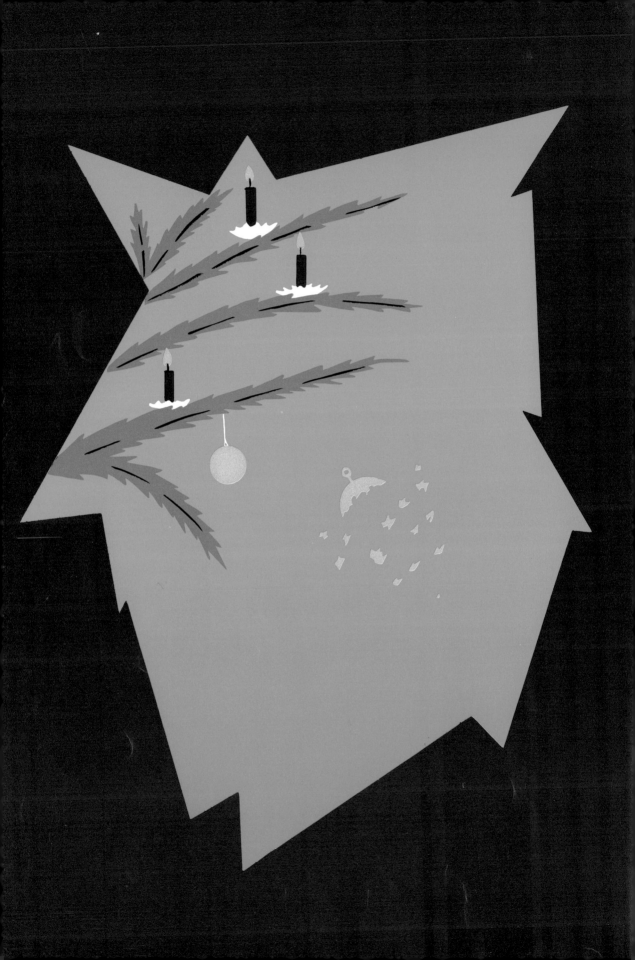

the sound of something brittle and
shining and full of air breaking into
a hundred little golden pieces?

NO

Was it

a big butterfly flying through the night?

NO

Was it

a happy elephant snoozing in a hammock?

NO

Was it

someone telling a secret?

NO

Was it

icicles freezing?

NO

Was it

a weather vane whistling in the winter wind?

NO

Was it

an old black crow?

NO

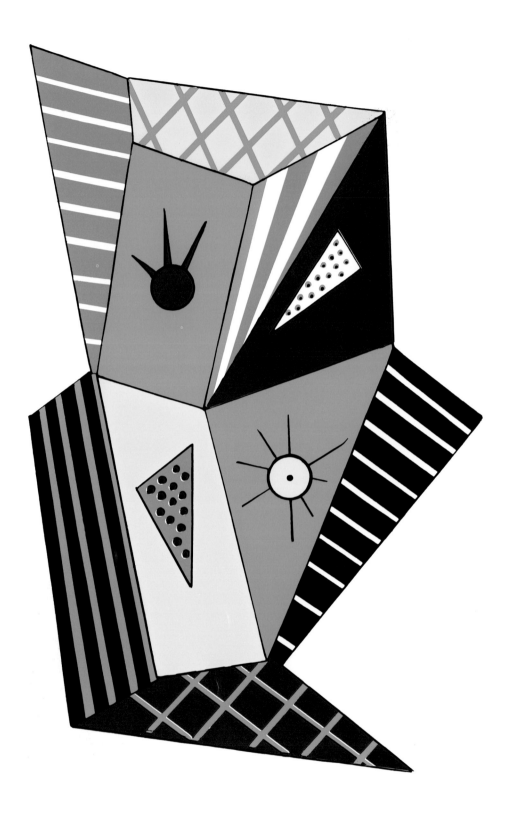

What do you think it was?

It was the snow falling out of the
sky, of course.

And Muffin caught a snowflake
on his little black nose and ate it
up.